OUTBURST

THE ALTERNATIVE

OUTBURST

PATRICK JONES

darbycreek
MINNEAPOLIS

Darby Creek
A division of Lerner Publishing Group, Inc.
241 First Avenue North
Minneapolis, MN 55401 U.S.A.

For updated reading levels and more information, look up this title at www.lernerbooks.com.

Cover and interior photographs © Jason Stitt/Dreamstime.com (girl);
© iStockphoto.com/joeygil (locker background).

Main body text set in Janson Text LT Std 12/17.
Typeface provided by Linotype AG.

Library of Congress Cataloging-in-Publication Data

Jones, Patrick, 1961–
    Outburst / by Patrick Jones.
        pages   cm. — (The alternative)
        Summary: After spending time in a juvenile detention center for a crime related to severe anger issues, seventeen-year-old Jada Robinson is sent to a foster home and enrolled in an alternative high school, and begins to move past her old life.
        ISBN 978–1–4677–3901–6 (lib. bdg. : alk. paper)
        ISBN 978–1–4677–4634–2 (eBook)
        [1. Anger—Fiction. 2. Foster home care—Fiction. 3. High schools—Fiction. 4. Schools—Fiction. 5. African Americans—Fiction. 6. Mothers and daughters—Fiction. 7. Letters—Fiction.] I. Title.
PZ7.J7242Ovd 2014
[Fic]—dc23   2013041392

Manufactured in the United States of America
1 – BP – 7/15/14

WITH THANKS TO ALLYSON, ANALEYSHA,
ARIANNA, BRITTNEY, KIARA, AND NAYALIE

-P. J.

THREE MONTHS EARLIER

"You always say you'll change, Jada, but I don't believe you!"

Jada pushed back hard against the harsh words with both hands. Her shove earned her another slap. She hardly felt the sweaty palm against her face. Her cheeks were already burning with anger, along with the rest of her.

Jada's first blow shut her critic's mouth; the second broke her jaw. The fists that followed knocked her to the ground, where Jada's kicks landed hard against soft flesh.

"How could you say that to me?" Jada

shouted, but there was no response. Her accuser was down and out. As Jada stared down, her body shook with all the familiar emotions. Like every time before, Jada felt anger, sadness, shame, and regret, but mostly fear. Always fear.

Jada bent down beside her bleeding victim. Softer now, through tears, Jada asked again, "Why did you say that to me?"

Jada knew there would be no answer. But she kept repeating the words as she fumbled for her phone and dialed. Soon, the sounds of sirens—not uncommon in her neighborhood—would blast through the St. Paul night. One siren would be the ambulance. The other would be a police car for Jada.

1

Dear Judge,

Thank you for placing me here in JDC for a little while so I could learn my lesson. I know I have made some bad choices in the past, but I've changed this time. It will be different if you let me go back to my mom and don't send me to foster care. If I go home, I will get involved in activities such as Girl's Club and teach young kids how to shoot hoops. But mostly I'll learn to control my anger when people disrespect me. I'll do whatever you tell me to do. I'm done fighting and causing problems at home with my mom. She's got enough problems being sick without me hurting her too. I'm sorry for breaking the law. I'll stop shoplifting, smoking weed, and acting out all angry. I'll do whatever it takes, even if means I got to stop hanging around with my friends who sometimes get me into trouble. So I'm asking you to give me one more chance.

I know it is hard to deal with kids like me and I understand that I have to follow the rules, so that is why I am writing this letter to you like my PO told me I had to. If you let me go home, then I will write a letter like this to my mom as well to apologize for what I did that caused me to get locked up again. If you just give me one last chance then I promise I'll control my anger and you won't see me back in this courtroom ever again. Please, please, please.

Thank you judge!!!!!

Jada Robinson

2

Jada squeezed the short yellow pencil in her hand. Writing with the tiny tool made her feel like a giant with her thick, tall frame. *I mean it this time,* she thought. *This time will be different.* She carefully folded the letter and put it in the envelope. She didn't need a stamp; she'd read it in person to the judge tomorrow. Jada hated speaking in front of people, especially adults with authority, but she was getting used to it. Just like she got more used to the colorless world of Ramsey County Juvenile Detention Center with every visit.

Back home, Jada was a color queen: lips, hair, nails, name it. Whatever she could change about herself, she would. Whatever she could shoplift from the Walgreens or Dollar Tree, she'd use and share with Kayla, Tamika, and Tonisha. They felt more like siblings to her than her two half-brothers, both of them full-on trouble. They'd both been in and out of the JDC many times. They'd all probably written the same letter—it wasn't even the first time Jada had written one—to the same judge.

Everything was gray in the JDC, aside from the faces, which mostly, like hers, were brown. Except in court, where the judges' faces were almost always white. And the judges never smiled, which made no sense to Jada, since judges had all the power and control, and the kids had none.

Jada picked up the *Free on the Inside* Bible that the chaplain had given her last Sunday. He'd asked if she had a favorite passage. Jada said Matthew 5:39, which her mother always told her she'd better learn to obey: turn the other cheek. Truth was, she'd never read the Bible. Nor had she read any of the books she took from the JDC library. She'd flipped through the hip-hop and sports magazines. *Lots of those stars got into trouble when they were kids*, Jada thought. *All I need is a break like them. All I need is one more chance.*

3

"Do you understand the rules of our home?" asked Mr. Markham, the balding foster father. He'd handed Jada the paper list almost the second he took custody of her, upon her release from JDC. She'd stared either at the paper or out the window the entire trip from Ramsey County Family Court to the driveway at the Markhams' house. "Once you've read them, then sign at the bottom of the page."

Jada shifted in the small seat in the un-air-conditioned old-school minivan. When she moved her feet, she heard a snap. Since the van's floor held a collection of small toys, plastic spoons, and cereal, Jada guessed there'd be little kids in the foster house. She'd liked having kids around in the past. But she didn't like that Mr. Markham—or other fake, white dads before him—called it a foster "home." It was a house, not a home. And unlike before, the judge said this wouldn't be a short-term placement. Three months, minimum.

"It's important that I know you understand the rules before we go into the house, for everyone's sake," Mr. Markham added.

Mr. Markham hadn't said much on the trip from the courthouse downtown to the house in the east St. Paul burbs, but it was more than Jada had said. She'd used all her energy—which wasn't much, since she couldn't sleep or eat or do much but worry while at JDC—to keep from crying at the judge's unfair decision. *If I don't cry*, Jada reasoned, *then I'm still in control.*

"If there's any section you don't comprehend, let me know."

Jada wanted to crumple up the papers and shove them down Mr. Markham's throat, so he'd feel what it was like to have people always choking you with their rules. But she knew a burst of anger like that meant a trip right back to JDC. If she blew this placement at the Markhams', Jada was pretty sure the judge would never let her go home.

"Gimme a pen and I'll sign the stupid thing," Jada muttered.

"When you ask for something in our house, we expect you to say please. Understand?"

"I need a pen, please."

Mr. Markham clicked the pen and handed it to Jada. "You'll do fine here." She wanted to jab it into his satisfied "I won" face.

Jada signed her name on the last page like she hoped to sign autographs for fans one day.

"I'm surprised you didn't want to ask about any of the rules," Mr. Markham started up again. Jada handed him back the pen. *I signed your stupid paper*, Jada thought. *Now just shut up.*

"Not all our girls like our rules. You saw there will be no makeup of any kind?"

Only girls? While it wouldn't be like her girls back home, maybe one or two would be nice.

Doesn't really matter, though, Jada thought. Her friends would never leave her, even if she did live way out in white land. She'd hit her girls up online as soon as she got inside. So what if she'd told the judge she wouldn't contact them? No way the law would find out. Besides, didn't they have real criminals to catch? Bangers shooting into houses and killing babies? They shouldn't be wasting time on her.

"Jada, did you even read the rules?" Mr. Markham said.

Jada paused. She didn't want to lie, but she couldn't be honest. "Most of 'em."

"You need to read and understand all the rules before you can enter our home."

"I didn't know all the words." *Plus I don't care about your rules,* she thought.

Mr. Markham nodded. "Your PO told us that you had reading problems and that you were behind in credits from missing so much school, so we're going to solve that in two ways. First, you'll be attending Rondo Alternative High School. You'll start after Labor Day. You'll be in tenth grade."

Jada said nothing. At seventeen, she should be graduating from high school, the first in her family to get that far. But she'd missed so much school and failed so many classes, she needed a miracle to still make that happen.

"And second, I'm giving you one of the best books in the world." Mr. Markham handed her a thick book.

"A dictionary?" Jada raised an eyebrow. She scanned the cover of the red book, with all the letters of the alphabet lined up A to Z in a row like good soldiers. That's what the world wanted: good soldiers, people to take orders. It didn't matter if it was teachers at school, crew leaders on the corner, Mr. Markham and his stupid list, or Jada's mom with her unfair rules.

"So if you don't know a word, you look it up." The book sat in Jada's lap. "It'll help you in school and in life."

Jada sat silent.

"We want you to succeed, but ultimately, that's your choice. Understand?"

That word again. With her left hand, Jada

pointed her middle finger at the letter F on the book cover.

"Jada, don't you have anything to say?"

With her right hand, Jada pointed her middle finger at the letter U. Then she looked up to meet Mr. Markham's stare.

4

"Jada, welcome to Rondo Alternative High School," said the dark-skinned black woman with curly hair and a big blue sweater. "I'm Mrs. Baker, the school principal. You've met Mr. Aaron," she said as she motioned to the older guy next to her with short gray dreads. He'd met her at the front door and walked her into the small office. "And this is Mrs. Howard-Hernandez," the principal continued, introducing a younger white woman who smiled at Jada.

One of me, three of them. Adults always got the odds, Jada thought as she yawned. No way was she getting up crazy early again. She hoped, since it was the first day, that it was a one-time thing. If not, it didn't matter if she learned these people's names and faces, 'cause she wouldn't see much of them until after ten.

"Normally, Jada, school starts at eight," the white woman said. Her short hair was blonde. *Probably fake like her smile*, Jada thought. "We wanted you to feel no pressure on your first day, so we asked you to come in early, to help you get acquainted."

"Thanks," Jada mumbled.

"I'm the language arts teacher, and I'll be your coach," Mrs. Howard-Hernandez continued. Jada wondered what she meant by *coach*. Her basketball coach back at Central High was the only coach who'd ever gotten her to listen or taught her anything. But Jada knew enough about alternative schools to know they had no sports teams.

"We're here to help you get a fresh start at our school," Mrs. Baker said. Jada noticed that the woman had a yellow folder on the desk. No doubt it held everything you always wanted to know about Jada Robinson's messed-up life but were afraid to ask. *They say you get a fresh start,* Jada thought, *except as soon as you show up, there's a yellow folder in some adult's hand, branding you.* She'd hated reading *The Scarlet Letter* in school last year, but that part of it had stuck with her.

"Now, you played sports—you're an athlete, right? So you know all about teamwork," Mr. Aaron said.

Jada nodded. She'd played her part in this scene many times. Adults talked about expectations and that nonsense; she nodded, smiled, acted polite like they needed, and then did what she wanted.

"We're a team. Our goal is to have you finish this year with enough credits so next fall you can enter as a junior. Do you think that's a reasonable goal?" Mrs. Baker asked.

Another nod directed at Mr. Aaron. He smiled, but Jada didn't give him one back.

"Like any team, everybody plays a role," Mrs. Baker continued. "Your role is the hardest because you're the point guard. You need to decide when to shoot, when to pass."

Man, I always shoot, Jada thought. They obviously hadn't read her file, because Jada played power forward. Point guard was for smart, short, scrappy white girls with no touch.

"And like any sport, there are rules, but mostly what we have here are expectations," Mrs. Baker said. Jada sank in her seat and waited for someone to hand her another rule book. "It's simple: show up on time, work hard, and give students, teachers and staff the respect that we'll all show you."

Jada sniffed and rolled her eyes.

"Mr. Aaron is the educational assistant, and he—" Mrs. Baker started.

"I set a mean pick," Mr. Aaron said, then laughed. When he laughed, his dreads bounced. "I'm here to watch out for you, make sure you succeed. You come to me first."

"For what?" Jada asked. *Ain't no adult watched out for me before*, she thought. Usually it was all talk.

"To avoid trouble. Many of our students have backgrounds similar to yours. They've had trouble with the law, as have people in their families," Mr. Aaron said. "So we understand."

Mrs. Howard-Hernandez spoke up softly. "We're interested in that history because it helps us—and you—understand your past decisions so you can learn from mistakes. We don't care about who you were, but who you are."

"And who you want to become," Mrs. Baker added.

Jada said nothing as she looked around the small office so she could avoid eye contact with these strangers who wanted to act like her friends. She hated that people always said she had to earn their trust, even though they expected her to trust them from day one.

"So, we'll help you with your schoolwork and whatever else we can," Mr. Aaron said.

Mrs. Baker took over. "We want you here, Jada, and we want you to succeed, but—"

Here it comes, Jada thought. *With every 'but,' there's an asshole.*

"If you show up not in shape to learn—and you know what we mean—we'll call home," Mrs. Baker said. "If it happens more than once, then we'll recommend a treatment program."

Jada felt like rolling her eyes. She had lots of problems, but *that* wasn't one of them.

"If you're violent toward other students or staff, we'll send you home," Mrs. Baker continued. "If it happens more than once, then we'll speak to your probation officer."

Jada knew what that meant: back to JDC.

"Finally, if you don't do the work, you need to tell us why." Mrs. Baker reached her hands across the table, palms up, like she wanted Jada to grab them or something. *That ain't happening, lady*, Jada thought. "Open up, let us know what's holding you back, and then we can all move forward together."

"Do you have any questions?" Mrs. Howard-Hernandez asked. Jada looked at the clock.

"When does school start again?" Jada held back yet another yawn.

"Eight," Mr. Aaron answered and laughed again. "I'll show you to your locker."

5

"So, how are things in your foster home?" asked Jada's probation officer, Mrs. Terry.

"Alright," Jada answered. *I've gone a whole week not acting out,* she thought, *and this is my reward: another old white person sitting behind a big brown desk, asking me questions like they really care about me.*

Jada crossed her arms, covering the fugly gray T-shirt. The social worker still hadn't gotten her clothes from home, and the stuff the Markhams bought for her was too cheap and too loose.

"I know it's an adjustment, but the structure the Markhams provide is crucial to helping you change your behavior. You need to control yourself and avoid those bursts of anger that cause trouble."

"Maybe," Jada mumbled. The less she talked, the less chance there was of saying something bad.

"The Markhams will hold you accountable. You know what that means, Jada?"

Jada nodded. Not only did she know what it meant, she'd written down the definition. Mr. Markham had made Jada go through the list of rules one by one and tell him what each of the big words meant. The ones she didn't know, like *accountable*, he made Jada look up in the dictionary. He said looking up the words and creating a word list was making her smart, but Jada thought the opposite. It made her feel stupid.

"They say you're getting along with the two other foster girls. That's good." Since Jada was the youngest, and her brothers never brought her nieces and nephews around, she wasn't used to being with younger kids, but it was actually kind of fun. It was the only fun she had at the Markhams', since everything else—having a phone, being online, watching cable, hanging out with friends—wasn't allowed. Instead, they'd eat together and play board games. *I don't need to play board games*, Jada thought. *I'm already bored and playing the Markhams' rules game.*

"And how about school?" Mrs. Terry continued. "How's that going?"

"Alright," Jada muttered.

"If you were a writer and got paid by the word, you'd starve." Mrs. Terry laughed at her own joke. Lots of white people behind desks did that, Jada had noticed.

"I don't know what you want me to say," Jada explained.

"Well, is Rondo better than Central?"

Jada nodded.

"Can you give me an example of how?"

"At Central, most of the teachers act like they care, but there's just too many kids," Jada explained. "I get it, because at Central the teachers gotta care about the good ones, the bad ones, and the ones in between. But at Rondo, all they got are us bad kids, so maybe—"

"Stop right there. You're not a bad kid," Mrs. Terry said. "You've made bad choices."

"Fine," Jada said. She'd heard it all before.

"So you think the teachers at the alternative school care more?"

"Seems like it, but maybe that's just because there's a lot less of us to care about," Jada answered. "At Central, we'd have like forty kids in a class, and I didn't even know half of 'em. What, those teachers have, like, six classes? How many kids is that?"

Mrs. Terry started to speak, but then stopped. "You tell me. What is forty times six?"

"I didn't come here to do math," Jada said, and Mrs. Terry laughed. "At Rondo, there's maybe a hundred in the school. I don't know everybody, but the people there seem alright."

"I'm glad to see that you're not online, and that you've not contacted your old friends, as you agreed to," Mrs. Terry said.

Jada looked at her wide-eyed. *How'd she know that?*

"Have you written the apology letter to your

mother like the judge required?"

Jada said nothing. Even with her new word list, she didn't know what to write. She could write "I'm sorry" in a hundred languages, but she doubted it would be enough.

"Look, while the judge was moved by your letter to him, he decided time away from your mom would be best for both of you," Mrs. Terry said. "Fighting at school, shoplifting, possession, truancy—your record was full of small stuff, but aggravated assault is a serious crime, especially—"

"Given the vulnerable nature of the victim," Jada repeated the judge's harsh words.

Mrs. Terry nodded and then paused. "Have you thought about after you graduate? It's early, but it's good to have a goal."

Jada sat up in her seat. For once that was something she liked to talk about. She started talking about playing in the WNBA or becoming an actress, but Mrs. Terry interrupted.

"Those are nice dreams, but I asked if you have any goals. Something more short-term, closer to home."

Jada felt like she'd had a shot blocked. Rejected. Her hands went back over her chest, and she slouched back in the chair.

"What does your mother do?" Mrs. Terry asked.

Not much anymore, Jada thought, but knew she couldn't say it. If she was ever going to get back home, Jada knew she'd need to show a little more respect, especially toward her mom.

Mrs. Terry answered her own question by checking her computer screen. "By my records, last time I spoke with her she worked third shift in a laundry."

Jada stared at the floor. "I don't wanna work in no laundry at midnight."

"If you don't stay in school, that's likely to be one of limited options. You're making progress, but if you mess up and don't get an education, then your mom's hard life could be your hard life. Is that the life you want?"

Biting her dry bottom lip, Jada flipped her street-stare at Mrs. Terry. "No."

"Let's have you focus on something between working in a laundry and winning an Oscar.

We'll talk about that next month when we meet. Now, before you go, you need to take a UA."

"Why?" The adult world was alphabet soup: UA, JDC, PO, CO. *FU*, Jada thought.

"Condition of your probation, I told you."

"You won't find anything."

"Then what's the problem?"

"Why don't you trust me?" Jada countered.

"Trust is earned." Jada thought all adults in her life should get T-shirts with those three words on them and point to the shirt every time they wanted to rub salt into her wounds.

"I smoked a little weed, everybody does that," Jada said. Problem was, Jada knew, she was high one time she was arrested, so they were always going to make her pee into the cup. If she'd been high and mellow the last time too, Jada thought, maybe things wouldn't have turned violent and ugly.

"The bathroom is down the hall." Mrs. Terry handed her the UA kit.

Jada wanted to throw it against the wall, but she took it. She wished she could get credit for making that good choice along with the bigger ones. "I'll do your garbage UA, but I ain't lying to you about being clean. It's the truth." She wasn't like a lot of girls back home. *Maybe I don't know forty times six*, Jada thought, *but I know real-world math*. Get high or drunk, get freaky, get pregnant, get a kid, and get a check. Rinse and repeat.

Jada's real-life math was different. Counting days in the JDC, subtracting doctor's bills from paychecks, measuring out her mom's pain meds, deciding what to lift from the store and what wasn't worth the risk. But somehow, it always added up to the same thing: peeing in a cup to prove herself to some PO.

"Slam dunk!" Jada yelled as the ball went through the hoop nailed up on the Markhams' garage. On her shoulders, Heather screamed in delight. "Feather, now it's your turn."

Jada bent down and carefully helped Heather off her shoulders. Then, just as carefully, she helped the younger sister, Feather, up. The two girls were small for their ages—seven and six— and couldn't shoot a basketball worth anything. Jada tried playing horse and other games with them, but the only way the girls could make a basket was sitting on her shoulders. It wasn't much of a game, but it was better than nothing.

Which was kind of how she felt in general about life at the Markhams'. With more rules than the Bible, and more Bibles in the house than other books, Jada toed the line under the Markhams' watchful eyes. She played along with their rules to avoid going back to JDC. She had her own room, but she missed her friends and her things from her old life. Mrs. Terry talked about making a home visit, but she'd told Jada she'd have to earn it. Typical adult behind a desk, she didn't say how, other than "marked improvement."

"Do me again!" Heather shouted after Feather completed her dunk. Jada's shoulders ached from carrying the girls, who seemed to be growing by the week. Jada could feel herself packing on the pounds at the Markhams' too, since there was always food, a lot of it, and all of it good. But she had to admit it wasn't bad coming home from school and knowing there would be dinner and people to eat with, instead of eating fast food all alone in front of the TV or her phone.

"Girls, ten more minutes, and then you need to get ready for church!" Mr. Markham yelled from the front door. Jada sighed. She didn't want to go to church. Again. What was with these people? Church on Sunday, then Sunday school afterward, and church and teens-only class on Wednesday. They also read from the Bible every night. It's not that Jada didn't believe in God. As she looked at her life and her mom's life, it just seemed like God didn't believe in them.

The younger girls ran inside, while Jada stayed in the driveway, shooting baskets. One after another a perfect shot, nothing but net. If she got back to Central next year, maybe she'd make varsity. Maybe she'd be a starter, and by her senior year, she'd get a college scholarship. Maybe. As she dribbled the ball, the bounces seemed to spell out that word: maybe, maybe, maybe. Nothing was certain, everything was maybe, hanging on her choices.

❁ ❁ ❁

"Wanna hit?" A rail-thin white girl in a pink hoodie motioned to the joint in her hand as they stood behind the church. Like Jada, the girl must've bolted from the teens-only program held right after the church service. As long as Jada was at the van to meet the Markhams in an hour, she'd be fine. Better than fine, now.

Jada took the joint into her hand, inhaled, and let the smoke fill her mouth.

"You new?" the girl asked. Jada liked her hair: long, dyed blond with pink stripes.

Jada returned the joint. The girl sucked it like an asthma kid with an inhaler.

"Were you at JDC last summer?" the girl asked as she handed the joint back to Jada.

Jada still said nothing. If the girl asked the question, she knew the answer. Jada inhaled and drifted. Her other stays had been short until Mom took her home, but not the last time. Over the summer.

"They got me for stealing a car," the girl said. "Stole my fosters' car with them in it!"

"What?" Jada asked. She now had a vague memory of the girl at JDC.

"They were teaching me to drive, and we got into it, like always." The girl sat on the grass behind the south side of the church, which faced the highway. She motioned for Jada to sit with her, but Jada keep her distance and stayed standing. "So I just kept driving. Hippies. They had one of those hybrids, so we made it almost through Iowa before it ran out of gas."

Jada handed back the joint, sat next to the girl, and tried to focus on her story.

"Then I got out and hitchhiked. Made it as far as Houston, Texas, but I came back."

"Why?"

"Like, who did I know in Texas?" the girl laughed, inhaled, enjoyed. "I ran away a hundred times, but I guess I always end up back up here. I'm in a foster out in Whitebury."

Jada laughed. She'd heard the nickname for Woodbury from her friends. The joke was that the suburb had a blackout once—but the cops made him get back in his car and leave.

"What's your name?" the girl asked, friendly. "Mine's Alicia."

"Jada. Like the actress."

Alicia offered the joint to Jada, but she waved it away. "More for me, Jada."

"I got to be careful. I have to do a UA with my PO."

"OK." The alphabet soup made both girls laugh. Jada smiled; it had been a long time since she'd really laughed. Back with her girls, all the time. Now, not so much.

"I better get back in there. Never know who's gonna snitch on you," Jada said. She brushed the grass from her ill-fitting, knock-off brand jeans. "I gotta stay clean, you know."

"For the UA?"

"No, for the M-O-M," Jada said. "I wanna get back home."

Alicia took the last hit. "Must be nice, to have a home." She buried the joint in the dirt. "Here's my number." Alicia wrote ten digits on Jada's left hand. "Hit me up."

"I don't have a phone right now," Jada confessed.

"Next Wednesday then," Alicia said. "We'll get our God on out here."

Jada laughed. So far she hadn't "found a friend in Jesus," as the Markhams vowed she would, but maybe she'd found a kindred spirit.

"So, what did you learn tonight?" Mr. Markham asked when Jada climbed into the van. Heather and Feather sat in the back seat, so Jada had the middle row to herself.

"You don't learn things in church." Jada snapped her spearmint gum, which Alicia had handed her. That, along with the some perfume samples she'd ripped out of fashion magazines at Walgreens, probably gave her enough to mask the weed stank.

Mr. Markham said nothing as he put the van into gear. He often opted for silence. Mrs. Markham talked a lot, but not so much to Jada, the girls, or her husband. She lived on her phone, talking to who knows who about political stuff. *As long as she doesn't talk to me*, Jada thought, *my prayers are answered.*

"I need to finish an essay on the computer when I get home," Jada said.

Mr. Markham sighed. "No screen time after 9:00 p.m.," he said. He didn't ask her about the letter to her mom that she'd started and stopped at least ten times since Sunday.

"I didn't get it done after school because I was playing with the girls," Jada snapped.

"Then you need to manage your time better," Mr. Markham said. "And make better choices."

Jada didn't argue because it got her no place. *There is no place for me*, she thought. *Not here, not home, not JDC.* Jada tried to fall asleep in the van because those thoughts did her no good. The more she thought, the nastier her mind got. It was like peeling off the wallpaper in a squat: ugly on top, but with even more hideous layers below.

7

"Can I use your phone?" Jada asked the thin mixed-race girl who stood smoking on the side of the road in front of Rondo.

The girl replied the same way Jada did when she was asked a question at school: just a blank stare.

Jada explained her no-phone situation to the girl, who she thought was named Jessica. Jada recognized her and remembered that she talked even less in class than Jada did.

Jessica motioned to the cig in her hand. Even outside, Jessica stood apart from everyone, near the road. The other smokers hung in the smoking area.

Jada didn't have a smoke to give in return for borrowing the phone. She opened up her purse to Jessica, but like her room at the Markhams', it was mostly empty.

Jessica took a step closer and shopped Jada's purse. She grabbed the nail polish from inside it even quicker than Jada had lifted it from the Walgreens shelf. Jessica put the polish in her pocket, handed Jada the phone, and said, "Just five minutes."

Before she closed the purse, Jada grabbed the paper where she'd written down Alicia's number. She dialed, but it went right to voicemail. "Damn!" Jada handed back the phone.

She saw Jessica almost smile, but not quite.

"You want some eyeliner next time?" Jada asked. Jessica nodded and tossed the cigarette butt to the ground.

Jada buried her smile. She'd wanted to hit somebody up for a phone since she had started at Rondo, but she couldn't get a read on most people. Like at all schools, there were cliques, and none of them seemed open to her. The Hispanic girls went their own way. The other black girls talked too much and too loud for Jada's taste, but the queen bee, Yvette, was the worst. Every morning at breakfast, she jumped to the front of line. Today Jada had pushed back—and pushed herself out of any chance of joining up with Yvette's group. Some of the white girls seemed okay, but Jada could tell most were troubled—and trouble—except maybe Jessica. No doubt she was troubled too, but it seemed like she meant no harm to anyone else. *Like me*, Jada thought.

◦ ◦ ◦

"Jada, a minute, please," Mr. Aaron said, just before the bell rang for fifth period. She was making an effort to be on time for classes, but in particular for biology with Mr. Hunter. Unlike a lot of the other teachers, who tried to act cool, Mr. Hunter was pretty strict. But at the same time, Jada thought his class was actually fun. Rather than just talking or reading, he made the students do lots of group projects and demonstrations and make PowerPoints. It was hard, but Jada was into the hands-on approach.

"What is it?" Jada asked. Mr. Aaron waved her into his small office. On Mondays and Wednesdays, Mr. Aaron and Mrs. Howard-Hernandez did a check-in with Jada, asking her how things were going and all that, but it was Thursday. Jada frowned.

"Sit down, please," Mr. Aaron said, and Jada complied.

"What did I do now?" Jada snapped. But she had known this was coming, so she hunkered down in the chair.

"What happened between you and Yvette this morning?" Mr. Aaron asked.

Since there were no adults around when it went down, somebody must've snitched to Mr. Aaron. "I don't like people pushing me, disrespecting me, and acting like I'm garbage."

"But pushing back just makes it worse. You need to come to us. Me, Mrs. Baker, Mrs. Howard-Hernandez . . . Everybody here cares about you. You know that's true, right?"

Jada took a deep breath, followed by another

and another, but said nothing. Mr. Aaron sat just as quietly. He sat across from Jada, eyes wide open and hands on the table. The ticking of the old clock on the wall filled the silence until Mr. Aaron finally spoke.

"While I understand that things didn't escalate, they could have, and the police would have been called. You would have violated probation, and you'd be back at the JDC."

"Maybe," Jada mumbled.

"And if that happens, then your chances of reaching your goals, like graduating from high school or going back home to live with your mom . . ." Mr. Aaron stopped talking, like it was a test and he wanted her to finish the sentence with the right answer. Jada stared at the white table.

"I have the incident report here." Mr. Aaron pushed a sheet of paper across the table. "I'd like to hear you tell your side of the story. Can you do that?"

"I got nothing to say . . ." Jada sighed like her lungs hurt. "'Cept it won't happen again."

"When you came here, we laid out our

expectations, but I forgot an important one: tell the truth. I don't care about *what* happened, but *why* it happened and what you learned from it."

Jada took the paper in her hand. She started to read it, but it was hard with tears from her eyes blurring the page. She handed the paper back to Mr. Aaron. "I'll try harder."

"No, tell me exactly what you'll do differently."

Jada wiped her eyes. "I don't know. Just tell me what you want me to say."

Mr. Aaron let out a long, slow breath. "You chose violence. Why?"

Jada answered the question by leaving the room, grabbing her stuff, slamming her locker door loud enough for everyone to hear, and walking, head down, away from the school.

8

"You got a car?" Jada asked Alicia outside the church.

Alicia exhaled. The pot smoke danced around Jada's head. "Maybe. Why?"

Jada wished she hadn't asked, but she didn't have any other options. The Markhams didn't live close to any buses. There was no way they or her PO would drive her. Most of the girls at Rondo didn't have cars of their own, and even if they did, they'd probably want something more in return than eyeliner. And she hadn't figured out the guys yet, but she didn't have the energy to risk making one think she was interested.

"Where do you need to go?" Alicia asked. Jada took a step away.

"I need to get to my mom's place," Jada answered.

Alicia laughed. "That's a mistake."

"I know I can't see her yet," Jada started. She filled Alicia in on being placed in foster care for at least three months after her last arrest, and how the judge ordered her to write an apology letter to her mom before going home.

"Why you want to mess up your probation?" Alicia laughed again. "I mean, it's not like I'd know *anyone* who'd do anything they weren't supposed to be doing." Alicia inhaled deeply.

Jada told Alicia about the letter to the judge and how he'd rejected her request. "But I actually meant what I said."

"It's easy to say you'll change, until you get back in your old life," Alicia said.

Jada thought about that. She wasn't skipping school, sleeping through class, or doing most of the things that got her in trouble in the past, maybe because she wasn't around her mom or her girls. She had to admit it was easier to be "responsible" for just herself, no one else. But it wasn't that simple. Nothing was. "I can't mess up. I don't know what they'll do to me if I do."

Alicia laughed so loud Jada thought people inside might have heard it over the Jesus music. "There's nothing they can do. They gotta house, feed, and clothe you. They can't kill you."

Jada wasn't laughing. "Might as well already be dead."

"Look, you ain't dead, you just ain't found the right way to live yet. Me neither." She offered the joint again to Jada, who turned it down. "Why you want to get to your mom's place?"

"I need my phone, some clothes, something decent to wear."

"You'd think with how the county rains money on foster parents, they'd spend it on us."

"Money?"

Alicia shook her head. "Trust me, ain't nobody taking in hard cases like us unless they're getting a check. Well, except maybe some of the people inside." Alicia nodded toward the church.

"I think the Markhams take in foster kids to save their souls."

Alicia nodded, inhaled, and exhaled.

"How many houses you been in?" Jada asked. She'd known kids at Central who lived in fosters, and she guessed a few at Rondo did too, but it wasn't something she wanted to talk about at school.

"More than I got piercings. Less than I got fingers and toes."

When Alicia finished the joint, Jada moved closer. "Why?"

"Why am I in a foster home?" Alicia snapped. "Why the hell do you think?"

Jada felt stupid for asking, for not knowing, and for making Alicia angry at her. She needed a ride and a friend, in that order. "Sorry, just asking."

Alicia shrugged and waved her hand in front of her face. Alicia didn't wear a lot of makeup, although she went heavy on the perfume, probably to mask the pot smell more than anything else. Alicia had this look like she could care less about interacting with most of the world. Something about how she spoke, dressed, and glared. Her eyes were off-limits signs.

"I got no dad, and my mom, well. You know." Alicia pointed with her right index finger inside of her elbow. "Heroin."

"Is she—"

"She OD'd when I was ten."

"I'm sorry."

"Don't be; I'm not," Alicia said. "Now I have a chance at a life. What's your mom's drug of choice?"

Jada was stunned by the assumption and how casually she'd asked. "She's on a lot of meds. She's sick. Lupus." That was something she'd yet to reveal to her "teammates" at Rondo. Although she figured the adults already knew and were just waiting for her to spill it to them in a tearful, life-changing moment.

"Sorry, is that why you're—"

"No."

"Then—"

"Can I have that ride?"

"Like I said, maybe," Alicia said. "If your mom's just sick, then why won't they let you live at home or even visit? I mean, she's not an unfit mother, or any of that social services crap?"

Jada weighed her choices, all of them wrong. "Could we go tonight?"

Alicia opened her purse and put on more perfume. "Give me your address, and I'll pick you up. My fosters lock up the doors at eleven, so I wait until one to sneak out. You can tell me more then."

9

"Hey, moo cow, wake up!" Jada felt her chair shake at the same time. Calvin's voice was booming at her in a mocking tone. She'd heard him insult other people yesterday like some dog marking his ground. *You push my buttons, fool,* Jada thought, *I'll knock you out.*

"You wanna make sure you're awake to eat lunch, moo cow."

Yesterday had been his first day at Rondo. He was an older, tall white twig with a face full of zits and whiskers. *If you don't shut up,* Jada thought, *today's gonna be your last on Earth.*

Calvin started making mooing sounds. Jada rubbed her eyes and looked around the room. She'd been late for school, and the rule at Rondo was if you were late for school, you couldn't just walk into a class and disrupt it. Instead, you went in this small unused classroom.

"Where's Mr. Aaron?" Jada mumbled to herself. She wasn't going to say a word to Calvin, not give him the satisfaction of showing she cared about a nasty word he said.

Calvin continued to moo, then stopped. "Wrong animal. You snore like a pig."

As Calvin started to oink, Jada yawned. She'd overslept, but that wasn't her fault. She'd sat on the front porch of the Markhams' until two waiting for Alicia, who never showed.

"Eat like a cow, snore like a pig, but I wonder do you suck like—"

Jada slapped the words out of Calvin's mouth. When she raised her hand again, he laughed and smiled like a kid who got the present he wanted for Christmas. Instead, she grabbed her bag and ran toward the exit. The school secretary shouted at her, but Jada didn't stop. Out of shape and out of breath, Jada got as far as the end of the parking lot before stopping. She slammed her book bag against the ground over and over. The force of it jarred her body, sending shock waves of pain from head to toe and tears bursting from her eyes.

"Jada!" It was Mr. Aaron, a few feet away and growing closer. Jada turned her back to him. She dropped the bag and used the sleeve of her hoodie to wipe her eyes clean.

"Jada." Softer now, almost a whisper as he stood behind her. Jada kept her head down and let her arms drop to her side. *Hug me, please just hug me*, she thought.

"What's wrong?" Mr. Aaron asked. No hug, but a hand on her shoulder. Good enough.

Jada paused. At Central, the worst thing was to snitch. Somebody did something do you, chances are you deserved it. You didn't tell on 'em; you got back at 'em. That was code of the school, the streets, and her home. And that had landed her at Rondo with the other rejects and at the Markhams' with the other unwanted kids. "I can't say."

"Jada, whatever you tell me, I won't tell anyone," Mr. Aaron said. Jada hated when adults lied, even if they did it for good reasons. She'd been around enough to know there were lots of things kids told adults that adults were required to share because of the law.

"Let me set the pick, Jada," Mr. Aaron said, hand still on her shoulder.

Jada turned away. She looked down the road left, in the general direction of the Markhams' house, south of the school. Like she was on the court, she pivoted and stared north, toward her real home, her mom's house. Finally, she looked at the school—not even really a school, but an old building attached to an ice rink—and started to speak. "Calvin."

"What about Calvin?"

Jada picked up her bag. As she walked into school she told Mr. Aaron about Calvin's words, her actions. When they reached the door, Jada said, "I thought about your question to me. Why I choose violence. But something about Calvin just gets at me. I want to learn from my mistakes."

Mr. Aaron held the door open. "Jada, if everybody learned from their mistakes the first time, then none of us here would have jobs. But you know what? That would be okay with me."

Once inside, Mr. Aaron directed Jada to the small conference room where she'd first met her team, and where she talked with them once a week. Mr. Aaron gave her a magazine to read while he made phone calls. Before she could finish the first article—a story about "having it all" with Halle Berry—Mrs. Baker and Mrs. Howard-Hernandez were in the room.

"Do they know?" Jada asked Mr. Aaron. He shook his head. He hadn't lied, so Jada thought she shouldn't either. Quickly, biting back emotion, she told the story. "I don't want him getting in trouble because I snitched. That just makes it worse. I'll handle it."

"By assaulting him again?" Mrs. Howard-Hernandez asked.

"No."

"Then how?" Mrs. Howard-Hernandez pressed. "What are you learning in anger management class?"

"The classes are full," Jada said. Just like going to therapy with her mom, the classes were another probation condition, but the stupid social worker hadn't come through, again.

"About this situation," Mr. Aaron said. "I doubt that Calvin would press charges."

Jada dropped the magazine. She'd heard that "won't press charges" lie before.

"That's not what matters, Jada," Mr. Aaron said. "What matters is how you responded. If you continue to respond to someone verbally assaulting you with violence, then you're trapped in a cycle. You have to change *your* response, because you can't change *their* behavior."

"You have to learn to walk away if someone calls you names," Mrs. Baker added.

"What if they hit me?" Jada asked. "I can't defend myself?"

The adults looked at each other like they didn't know who should answer. Finally, Mr. Aaron spoke. "That's why you're here, Jada, to learn different strategies. The ones you've used in the past, well, where did they get you? JDC, foster care, here."

"But *she* started it!" Jada yelled and then shut her mouth, like she should've done all along. This wasn't about Calvin, and they knew it; it was about what happened with her mom.

10

"I have a report here from your school," Mrs. Terry said, once Jada had sat down for her PO meeting. "I'm pleased. Are you?"

Jada didn't know how to answer, but she knew she'd say thank you to Mr. Aaron. He had told her he'd let recent incidents slide, since her willingness to talk out issues with staff was more important than punishments. Mrs. Terry wouldn't be pleased if the school had mentioned her slapping Calvin.

"Your grades are up, you're earning credits, and you're staying out of trouble," Mrs. Terry continued. Jada sat a little taller.

"And a good report from the Markhams. They say you're getting along well with other children and not acting disrespectfully, and they seem pleased by your eagerness to attend church."

Jada almost burst out laughing. "Church is great." *If they only knew*, Jada thought.

"But I've also spoken with your county social worker, and there are some issues with—"

"The issues are with her," Jada shot back. "She's not doing nothing for me."

Mrs. Terry seemed amused by Jada. "Jada, let's focus on you and your mom—"

"She won't show up for therapy," Jada whispered. "My mom don't want me back."

Mrs. Terry shook her head, all self-righteous. "I've spoken with your mother and—"

Jada took a deep breath and then flinched when she asked the question, "How is she?"

"She wants you back, Jada, if you've made real changes, and from these reports, it—"

Jada leaned closer. "No, how is she? Her lupus."

Mrs. Terry glanced down. "We didn't talk about that specifically, but she seemed to be doing all right."

Jada felt rage building, toward Mrs. Terry for not caring, not asking about Jada's mom's health. Toward her mom, for being sick, for missing out on so much of Jada's life, and for one day, maybe soon, dying and leaving Jada alone. But mostly toward herself for acting out angrily and doing what she did to her mother.

"Are you okay?" Mrs. Terry asked.

Jada didn't answer because she couldn't figure out what to say. She was anything but okay. She missed her mom but didn't miss the fights between them. As exhausted as Jada was with school at Rondo, it was nothing like she felt helping her mom when she was sickest. A disease like lupus sapped everybody's strength, leaving nothing but fear and worry.

"And the letter. How is that coming?" Mrs. Terry asked.

"I haven't started it," Jada mumbled.

"Why not?"

Jada looked at the photos on Mrs. Terry's desk. None of kids. Just her, some dork, and skis. How could any of these people with their desks and degrees understand anything? They didn't have a mother who was dying. They didn't have people all around them without money or hope. "You wouldn't understand."

"Jada, that's a condition of going home."

"It's just a letter."

"No, Jada, it is an apology," Mrs. Terry said slowly. "You need to apologize for what you did to your mother. You need to admit your behavior was wrong and—"

"I already told the judge all that," Jada said. "And you said I'm doing better."

Mrs. Terry leaned over her desk. "You need to write the words down so your mom can get it straight from you. You need to write the words, 'Mother, I'm sorry for assaulting you.'"

Jada put her hands over her eyes, as if they could be dams against the tears.

Mrs. Terry continued. "You need to let her know how you're going to handle challenges differently going forward. Then it's up to her to accept the apology and trust that you've changed, or not."

11

"She started it!" Heather shouted. Jada stood between Heather and Feather so they wouldn't hit each other. They'd been double Dutching in the Markhams' driveway, in the sweet bit of free time after dinner but before Wednesday night church.

"It's her fault!" Feather shouted back.

"Keep your voices down." Jada pointed at the foster house.

Heather tried to push past Jada. "But—"

"You get into a fight, and they'll keep you two here forever. Is that what you want?"

Neither of the girls spoke. "That's what I thought," Jada said. She didn't know why the girls had been sent to the Markhams' and never asked. People's troubles were nobody else's business.

"Why don't we play dunk basketball instead?" Jada asked. Heather and Feather both bolted for the garage to get the basketball, leaving Jada alone with her thoughts. Her mom had never lived anyplace with a big driveway, complete with a basketball hoop, and her half-brothers never invited Jada to the park to play. Jada wondered what growing up would've been like if life had been less hectic, without all the moves, without her half-brothers always in trouble, and without her mom's lupus. Life didn't need to be easy—just not so hard all the time.

"Me first!" Heather shouted when she returned with the ball. Feather said nothing.

"You should let your sister go first for once," Jada said softly. "How about it?"

Heather clutched the big basketball to her chest and stared at Jada. "No."

Jada crouched down, got eye to eye with Heather. "Heather, do this for me."

Heather bounced the ball once, twice, but then passed it to her sister. Feather grabbed the ball, climbed on Jada shoulders, and dunked it. Everybody cheered. *If I can get them not to be angry at each other*, Jada thought, *maybe I can do the same for myself.*

◦ ◦ ◦

"Is her car in the driveway?" Alicia asked as they drove down the badly lit street in east St. Paul. Alicia had spent the drive apologizing for no-showing before, when she got caught sneaking out. Jada accepted the apology and the ride.

"My mom doesn't have a car," Jada answered.

"How will we know if she's home?" Alicia asked. She parked the car near the driveway. Jada thought Alicia seemed pretty calm, but that could just be the weed.

"Watch the light." Jada pointed at the corner front window, where a bright line shone. "When she turns it off, she's done reading and ready to fall asleep. We wait 'til after that."

"How do you know she won't wake up?" Alicia asked.

"She's on painkillers for her lupus," Jada answered. "They knock her out good."

"What's lupus?" Alicia asked. She had more questions than a court-appointed lawyer. Most of the time, Jada didn't like to tell people about her mom's sickness or her other troubles. Talking with Mrs. Terry and other adults never helped. But Jada wondered if Alicia might actually understand.

"She's in pain all the time," Jada started. "Her joints hurt, but she'd only take her pain pills if she had to, because she doesn't want to end up a junkie like my Aunt Trina . . ." She talked until her mom's light went off, and she didn't stop until Alicia told her that she needed to get home, so they had to make their move.

"Is there a key or something?" Alicia asked.

Jada shook her head.

"Then how are we getting in?" Jada didn't answer. She just walked toward the house.

Once they were standing together in the small, dirt-filled lot behind the house, Jada said softly, "You know what I like about you, Alicia?"

"I thought it was my weed, but . . ."

Jada laughed. It had been so hard not to get high. "That you're skinny." She picked up a stray piece of wood from the rotting porch and jammed it under a back window. When she pushed down on the wood, she got enough leverage to lift the window a few inches.

◦ ◦ ◦

The old floors creaked as Jada made her way through the house. She'd left Alicia by the back door, just in case. The door to her room wasn't locked; it couldn't be, since Jada had knocked out the lock and ripped the door off the hinges during her last night in the house.

Jada flipped on the light, and the single lightbulb shone over her. It reminded her of the booking room at JDC. She knew she never wanted to see that place again.

With snoring coming from the other room, Jada took her time finding the things she needed: phone, clothes, and makeup. In a drawer, she found her photo album with lots of pictures of her with her mom from back in the day. All her most recent photos were on her phone.

Jada put the phone in her pocket and jammed the charger and everything else into two pillowcases. Since the room was pretty much as she'd left it that last night, she doubted her mom would notice. *Does she even notice I'm gone?* Jada wondered. *Does she miss me at all? Does she forgive me?* Her mom hadn't visited her at JDC, nor had she shown up at the sentencing hearing. It wasn't her mom's fault, Jada knew—she had been in the hospital. That part wasn't her mom's fault either. Jada couldn't even blame the lupus. She could only blame herself for the burst of rage that exploded and the fury of punches she threw that broke her mom's jaw.

12

Is this a test? Jada thought. She looked around the table at the team she'd been assigned to for a group project in biology, her favorite class at Rondo. Jessica, who never said a word, Calvin, who never said a kind word, and Yvette, who never stopped talking about her fabulous life long enough for anyone else to speak. All three stared back at Jada with equal suspicion.

"This is your final project and accounts for one-third of your grade," Mr. Hunter said as he handed a sheet of paper to each table. He tended to drone on, but Jada forced herself to listen.

She'd thought about what Mrs. Terry had said about having a goal somewhere between working the night shift in a laundry and winning an Oscar. Jada knew the only thing she really liked in school was science. It wasn't just reading, but actually solving problems. She knew that scientists solved problems—like curing diseases.

"Each table will choose a topic from this list, related to the concepts we've covered this semester, to research and present. Discuss and decide on one that all four of you agree on," Mr. Hunter continued. "While you'll work together on all aspects of the project, each of you will have a specific role. One person will present to the class, one will create a Power-Point, one will demonstrate an aspect of the topic, and the fourth will design a poster. Questions?"

"Jessica should present!" Yvette said. Calvin laughed, but Jada said nothing. Jessica, of course, also said nothing. Yvette looked satisfied with herself. "I'm going to design a poster that will blow y'all away," she said.

"I'll do the demonstration. Maybe bring in some gunpower and really blow 'em away!" Calvin said. Jada tried to ignore Calvin, which was easy because she was focused on the list of topics in front of her. There it was: *pathology*—the study of diseases.

"We're supposed to decide together," Jada said. "Who put you in charge, Yvette?"

Yvette snapped her gum. "You got a problem with me? You wanna go again?"

Jada avoided eye contact.

"I'm all for a catfight," Calvin said. "Let's get it on."

Yvette started to stand up. "After school, outside," Jada hissed back. Yvette sat.

"Our topic should be why some girls are hot and others not," Calvin said, smirking. Yvette started squawking back at Calvin, both of them talking over each other.

"Well, I'm glad to see at least one group engaged in hearty debate and scientific inquiry," Mr. Hunter said as he strolled over to Jada's table. "So, what topic have you chosen?"

Jada sat up and spoke clearly. "Pathology,

the study of disease, and we'll do one disease in particular. Lupus."

"We didn't agree to nothing, she's just talking," Yvette said. "I think we should—"

Jada turned, flashed a hard street-stare at Yvette, and turned back toward Mr. Hunter. "No, that's the topic. Calvin is doing the demonstration. Yvette will do the poster."

"And who will be presenting for your group?" Mr. Hunter asked.

Jada looked at Jessica. For once, Jessica's face wasn't down on the desk. Instead, she looked up at Jada, her eyes pleading. "I'll do that. Jessica will do the PowerPoint."

Jessica mouthed the words *thank you* as Mr. Hunter walked over to the next group.

"I don't know nothing about lupus," Yvette said. "And I don't care. You shouldn't—"

"It's a disease that causes people to be in a lot of pain," Jada said.

"I'll tell you another one that does that, and you're gonna learn about it after school," Yvette said. "It's called my fist in your ugly, fat face, and there ain't no cure for that."

After the last bell, Jada gathered her things.

"Where are you going, Jada?" Mr. Aaron said. Jada said nothing. Mr. Aaron put his hand on her shoulder like he wanted to stop her. "Jada, you've come far in just a little time with us. Don't risk it. Is it worth it—going back to JDC? Not going home to your mom?"

"How do you know?" Jada asked. "Who told you?"

"I can't say."

No way Yvette or Calvin said anything, so it had to be Jessica who spoke up to protect Jada, just like Jada had done for her.

She looked at the floor and then dropped her bag. "I hafta do this."

"We can't allow a fight on school grounds."

Jada nodded, picked up her bag, and headed for the parking lot. Yvette and her crew were there, waiting near the end of the lot.

"Time to end this!" Jada yelled as she walked toward Yvette. Mr. Aaron followed behind. "You go around thinking you're better than everyone else, but you're not."

"So, what you going to do about it?" Yvette snapped back.

Jada glanced past Yvette, at the road behind her. She set down her bag, which held her word list, the dictionary that the Markhams made her carry, and a picture of her mom. Jada stared at Yvette, smaller than her but with a way bigger mouth.

"I'm not fighting you on school grounds," Jada said. "I'm not getting suspended."

"Fine by me." Yvette stomped toward the road. A crowd began to follow the two girls and stopped a few feet from Yvette. Jada stared at Yvette. Then she shook her head, picked up her bag, and started walking.

"Where you going?" Yvette said. Jada didn't turn around; instead, she just turned and headed toward the Markhams'.

13

Jada sat in her room at the Markhams', staring at her phone. She only had a few minutes left on it, so she had to decide how to spend them. She'd thought that the second she got it, she'd hit up her old friends—until she looked at the list of missed calls. There were none from Kayla or Tamika, and only one from Tonisha. Had they abandoned her? Had they heard what she did to her mom?

"Jada, you need to get ready for church!" Mr. Markham shouted from the bottom of the stairs. She tucked the phone deep into her jeans, since the Markhams didn't know about the phone and wouldn't approve of her having it, how she got it, or any of Jada's friends. Even if Jada called Tonisha, she didn't know how they'd get together, since Tonisha didn't have a ride.

Jada walked slowly down the stairs, remembering how quickly she'd run up them when she first got to the Markhams'. Running from her own life, her choices. She'd stood up for herself with Yvette by walking away. Now, she'd have to face another pass-fail test.

"Can you please pick me up after church?" Jada asked as politely as possible.

"I always do. Why are you asking?" Mr. Markham was good at answering Jada's questions with another question. He'd make a great probation officer, cop, or judge.

"No, I don't want to go to the after-church teen thing anymore."

"It's very important that you attend."

Jada knew she couldn't tell Mr. Markham the real reason: she wanted to avoid Alicia. She wanted to avoid not just the urge to get high, but the stronger urge to ask Alicia to drive her to see her old friends or check on her mom. Alicia was a new friend with a path to Jada's old life. "I've got schoolwork with the end of the quarter. I want to get an A for once."

"You'll have plenty of time to study after," Mr. Markham said.

"It's more than just that, I don't want to go any more," Jada countered.

"You don't get to make that decision."

"Why not? It's my life!" Jada yelled. So many times she'd gotten close to raising her voice with the Markhams but held back. She was glad she'd walked away from Yvette, but she was going to take this battle head-on.

"We're responsible for you, not just giving you a home but—"

"This is a house!" Jada shouted. "It's not my home."

"Until the judge says differently, it is your home. And you'll do as we say, and we say that you're going to attend the after-church class. Understand?" Mr. Markham said, his voice raised.

This is more like it, Jada thought. She and her mom never just talked about stuff—they went right into yelling. Next was throwing things, hitting things. Then hitting people. Jada felt rage building up inside her. Then she remembered her mom's broken face, and the air went out of her.

Jada calmed her voice. "Why don't you give me this?" she said. "I've done everything else you've told me to do. Why can't I get some credit for that? I've changed, and you—"

Mr. Markham's harsh laughter cut Jada off. "I've heard that so many times."

"But I mean it this time."

"They all say it, they all mean it—that is, until they get back to the streets, and then . . . "

"Why don't you believe in me?" Jada couldn't help raising her voice again.

Mr. Markham shook his head and turned his back. "I believe you're strong, but the streets are stronger. They always have been, and that's why we'll always have this home."

When Mr. Markham started to walk away, the memory snapped into place like a Lego. Her mother had said, more or less, the same words to her the night that Jada had lost it. It was one thing for rent-a-parents not to believe in you, but Jada couldn't stand her own mom saying those things about her. *I'm not my brothers, I'm not my friends, and I'll prove it*, she thought.

"Listen, Mr. Markham, I'm sorry for yelling," Jada said. His back was still to her. "Let me show you that you're wrong."

Mr. Markham turned around. He looked annoyed. "How?"

Jada dug her right hand deep into her pocket. "Look, I did something bad. I got someone to take me to my mom's house, and I got this." Jada showed him the phone.

Mr. Markham's eyes blazed with anger.

She opened it. "But look, I haven't called anyone. I was tempted—like you said, the streets are strong—but look, I'm stronger. I want to go home, but not back to my old life."

"Who took you to your mom's house?"

"I'm not snitching."

"Does this have something to do with not wanting to go to the teen class anymore?"

Jada nodded but still wouldn't say anything.

"Was it someone in the class at church?"

Since there were twenty-five kids in the class, no way Mr. Markham could figure out who it was. "Yes, but that's all I'm gonna say."

"Well, you'll be held accountable for that. But I'm glad you told me. That's good."

Jada nodded. For once, she wanted to be held accountable. *He can't take much of anything away*, she thought, *because I don't have nothing here I care about.*

"Jada, don't let fear control you."

"I'm not afraid of anything."

"Yes, you are," Mr. Markham said softly, like he cared.

Jada shook her head. "What am I afraid of?" She flashed him a street-stare. He blinked.

"I think you're afraid of losing your mom," Mr. Markham said.

Jada felt the tears welling up in her eyes and tried to fight it.

"For your punishment, you'll spend more time on schoolwork and start your letter to your mom, beginning tonight." Mr. Markham smiled. "I'll pick you up right after church."

14

Calvin didn't have his part of the presentation ready, which led to harsh words between him and Yvette. When Mr. Hunter told him to sit down, he lost it and started calling everyone names, including the staff. Jada just sat, smiled, and waited. Once Calvin had been escorted out of the room, Mr. Hunter told Jada to continue with the group's presentation.

She walked slowly to the front of the class. Yvette still sneered at her, as always, but Jada thought it was an act, since Mr. Hunter had praised Yvette's poster. Jessica showed her respect by keeping her head off her desk as Jada started to speak.

"Lupus is a disease in which the body attacks its own healthy tissues and organs," Jada read from the paper in front of her. "It can damage the joints, skin, kidneys, and other parts of the body. African American women are three times more likely to get lupus than white women, although it affects men and people of all races as well. African American women tend to develop lupus at a younger age and have more severe symptoms than white women." She was glad there was a lectern that she could rest the paper on so she didn't have to hold it. She hid her shaking hands in her pockets.

"Let me show you what I mean. Jessica, next slide," Jada said. Jessica clicked the mouse. A picture of Jada's mother appeared on the screen, looking happy and healthy. "That's my mom on the day I graduated from junior high."

"She's pretty," Yvette said. Jada smiled. She figured, since she'd never get an apology from Yvette for hassling her, this was Yvette's way of smoothing things out between them.

"That was before she got lupus," Jada said. "This is her now."

Another click, another photo. The classroom sounded like twenty tires going flat at the same time as students gasped. Jada stared at the photo. It showed her mom at the worst point of suffering from her lupus symptoms—skin covered in rashes, a swollen face, and patches of hair loss. But it wasn't the worst photo for Jada. That was the photo the judge had made her look at, the one of her mother after Jada beat her up.

Partly, she felt guilty for hitting back so hard when her mom slapped her. But it felt even worse to remember the reason: knowing her mom didn't believe in her. That hurt more than anything. It was like her mom had already abandoned Jada, even before the lupus would force her to.

"Look, those words I just read," Jada said, desperate not to cry in front of everyone. "I copied them off the Internet. I'm sorry, but I wanted you all to understand the disease better than I could write about it. So those are the facts, but now let me tell what it's like to live with a person with lupus. My mother is in pain most of the time. She has trouble concentrating and remembering. And she's tired all the time, so living with her, taking care of her, is hard. She . . . "

❊ ❊ ❊

Jada finished the presentation in tears. Mr. Hunter gave her permission to leave the class and called Mr. Aaron, who met Jada by the conference room door. He opened it and let her inside without saying a word. Sobs were coming hard from deep within her. Mr. Aaron handed her some tissues and let her cry, with one steady hand on her quivering shoulder.

After the bell rang for the next class, Jada remained seated. "Could I use your phone?" she asked Mr. Aaron. She'd seen kids ask before, and Mr. Aaron usually said no.

"Who do you want to call?" he asked.

Jada told him and said, "Could you get Mrs. Baker and Mrs. Howard-Hernandez to join us?" Mr. Aaron nodded and left the room. Jada dug into her purse and found the bent-up business card. She waited until Mr. Aaron and the other members of her team returned before she dialed the number. They'd all had her back, both protecting her and pushing her. So Jada wanted them all there as she took a long overdue leap forward.

"Mrs. Terry, it's Jada," she said. "I'm ready to write the letter to my mom."

15

Dear Mom,

I'm sorry it has taken me so long to write this letter. I didn't know what to say or how to say it. But also, when I wrote it, I wanted to mean it. I wanted to write it not because I was told to, but because I wanted to and I knew every word was true.

I shouldn't be treating you so disrespectful, after everything we've gone through and what you are going through because of the lupus. Sometimes I think I acted that way because I wanted to push you away, so when you die, it won't hurt so much. I think that I listened to my friends 'cause I thought they'd *be there for me forever, and you won't. But I'm glad I got put in this foster house for a while. I think I've learned my lesson.*

I don't know if you believe me when I say I'm changed, but if everybody lets me come home, then I'll show you, I'll show everyone. I know that I have to be accountable (look at me, using big words), but also that it's better just not to make bad choices. But it's not like you got a choice—you just got sick. I hate how it affects you, and me. I remember the first time I heard you moanin so bad that I called an ambulance. Before it came, do you remember how I rubbed your knees like somehow I could make the pain go away? But all I do is bring you pain. I'm sorry. Why does God make you suffer with being sick? I've prayed that you'll get better. Like how you prayed that I'd stop getting in fights at school or hanging with the wrong people.

I know you have no reason to believe me, but if you let me come home, you'll see your prayers were answered. I am so ashamed at what I've done and how much I've hurt you. I'm sorry for assaulting you. Please forgive me, Mom.

I was scared to come home before, 'cos I thought

I'd be the same. But I'm not. I know I can't be acting all angry all the time, driving everybody away, especially you. It doesn't get me where I want to go, which is home. I know it ain't going to be easy, but I want us to get through this together.
Your loving daughter,
Jada

"It's good to hear your voice," Jada's mother said. The sound of her mom's voice was sweet, even booming out of a speakerphone in a drably painted Rondo office.

"I'm glad you could join us, if only by phone," Mrs. Baker said. Seated at the table were Mrs. Howard-Hernandez, Mr. Aaron, and Ms. Terry. The county social worker was with Jada's mom.

"We've got a lot to cover," Mrs. Terry said. "Where do we want to start?"

"School," Jada said quickly. "I want to stay here at Rondo."

"At the rate you're going, you'll earn enough credits to transfer—" Mrs. Terry said.

"Doesn't matter, I want to stay here," Jada replied. "I need my team."

Mr. Aaron laughed. "We've got your back."

"Jada, if that's what you want, we can make it happen," Mrs. Baker said. "You certainly have done much better in our environment."

She knew that word—it was on her word list. That list, her basketball games with Heather and Feather, and home-cooked meals were about all Jada would miss at the Markhams'. She wouldn't miss Mr. and Mrs. Markham, though. She wasn't angry, but she realized they wouldn't miss her either. She was another kid they thought they'd set straight. *Truth is*, Jada thought, *I did all the work. They just set the rules. We both did our parts.*

"I'd like to switch coaches, though," Jada said softly. "Mrs. Howard-Hernandez is nice, but you're all into books and reading, and I'd rather have Mr. Hunter. I want to study biology."

"No offense taken. The world needs plenty of scientists and—"

"Doctor. I want to be a doctor who does research," Jada said.

"You have to shoot the three-pointer when you're young," Mr. Aaron said. Maybe, for a girl from the hood, doctor was a three-point shot. But maybe the people around the table and on the end of the phone would be like Jada with Heather and Feather. They'd carry her on their shoulders to get the slam dunk.

The adults talked among themselves, mainly Mrs. Terry and Mrs. Baker. Jada didn't hear her mom say much, but that was okay. They'd have lots of time to talk soon enough.

"Jada, there's an Alternative School Academic Olympics," Mr. Aaron said. "We'd like you, Jessica, and Yvette to enter your presentation— that is, if you're willing to tell your story again."

Jada stopped to think before she answered. "Yeah, I am." Maybe it was actually helpful, she thought, not to let stuff bottle up or keep your trouble to yourself, but to share it. "Is it okay with them?"

"Yvette seemed excited about it—you know she doesn't mind the spotlight," Mr. Aaron said.

"What did Jessica say?" Jada asked.

Mr. Aaron smiled. "She said 'yes.'"

"Out loud?" Jada asked, and her team laughed.

"What was your presentation about, Jada?" her mother asked.

"You, Mom, it was about you, and how brave you are for living with lupus."

There was silence on the other end of the phone for a few seconds. Then Jada thought she heard her mom crying. *And for once*, she thought, *these just might be tears of joy and pride.*

"Jada, I'm not that brave," her mom said. "I'm just a mother doing her best. You're the brave one."

Jada felt Mr. Aaron's hand on her shoulder as tears welled up in her eyes. His hand felt big, safe, and strong, like her mom's hands used to feel, and would again when Jada returned home.

"Don't cry, Jada," her mom said. "I believe in you."

AUTHOR'S NOTE

In addition to writing about teens in alternative schools, I also work with teens in the course of a nine-to-five job. The idea for this book came directly from my work with a juvenile detention center (JDC). The letters at the start and end of this novel are based on actual letters I found in a book at the JDC, but everything else, including the names, is fiction.

Outburst looks at one example of a young person in the correctional system who is placed in foster care. The rate of overlap between the two systems is high. According to a brief by the Brookings Institute:

A recent study of a Midwest sample of young adults aged twenty-three or twenty-four who had aged out of foster care . . . had extremely high rates of arrest and incarceration. 81 percent of the long-term foster care males had been arrested at some point, and 59 percent had been convicted of at least one crime. This compares with 17 percent of all young men in the U.S. who had been arrested, and 10 percent who had been convicted of a crime. Likewise, 57 percent of the long-term foster care females had been arrested and 28 percent had been convicted of a crime. The comparative figures for all female young adults in the U.S. are 4 percent and 2 percent, respectively.[1]

However, each child in foster care and each person in the correctional system has his or her own unique story.

It is always tricky to write about a different culture and gender. In this book, I tried to tell one girl's story—not to depict all people of any gender, race, or background. In addition to my years of experience working with African American girls in the correctional system, I shared this book with three girls at one correctional facility. They read and reacted to it, letting me know what I got wrong so I could make it right. So, special thanks to KM, KA, and SC.

Finally, as with all the books in The Alternative series, students and staff at South Saint Paul Community Learning Center read and commented on the manuscript, in particular John Egelkrout, Mindy Haukedahl, Kathleen Johnson, and Lisa Seppelt.

[1]Nicholas Zill, "Adoption from Foster Care: Aiding Children While Saving Public Money," Center on Children and Families Brief #43, May 2011, http://www.brookings.edu/~/media/research/files/reports/2011/5/adoption%20foster%20care%20zill/05_adoption_foster_care_zill.pdf.

ABOUT THE AUTHOR

Patrick Jones is the author of more than twenty novels for teens. He has also written two nonfiction books about combat sports, *The Main Event*, on professional wrestling, and *Ultimate Fighting*, on mixed martial arts. He has spoken to students at more than one hundred alternative schools, including residents of juvenile correctional facilities. Find him on the web at www.connectingya.com and on Twitter: @PatrickJonesYA.

THE ALTERNATIVE

FAILING CLASSES.
DROPPING OUT.
JAIL TIME.

When it seems like there are no other options left,
Rondo Alternative High School might just be the
last chance a student needs.

BARRIER
PATRICK JONES

BRIDGE
PATRICK JONES

CONTROLLED
PATRICK JONES

OUTBURST
PATRICK JONES

TARGET
PATRICK JONES

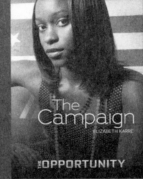

SOUTHSIDE HIGH

ARE YOU A SURVIVOR?

The Alliance

Bad Deal

Beaten

Benito Runs

Dance Team

Deadly Drive

The Fight

Full Impact

Overexposed

Plan B

Recruited

Shattered Star

Check out all the books in the

SURVIVING SOUTH SIDE

collection